RIDER WOOFSON

GHOSTS AND GOBLINS AND NINJA, OH MY!

BY WALKER STYLES ● ILLUSTRATED BY BEN WHITEHOUSE

WITH GRAHAM ROSS

LITTLE SIMON

New York   London   Toronto   Sydney   New Delhi

LITTLE SIMON

An imprint of Simon & Schuster Children's Publishing Division
1230 Avenue of the Americas, New York, New York 10020
First Little Simon paperback edition July 2016
Copyright © 2016 by Simon & Schuster, Inc.
Also available in a Little Simon hardcover edition.
All rights reserved, including the right of reproduction in whole or in part in any form.
LITTLE SIMON is a registered trademark of Simon & Schuster, Inc., and associated colophon is a trademark of Simon & Schuster, Inc. For information about special discounts for bulk purchases, please contact Simon & Schuster Special Sales at 1-866-506-1949 or business@simonandschuster.com. The Simon & Schuster Speakers Bureau can bring authors to your live event. For more information or to book an event contact the Simon & Schuster Speakers Bureau at 1-866-248-3049 or visit our website at www.simonspeakers.com. Designed by Laura Roode.
The text of this book was set in ITC American Typewriter.
Manufactured in the United States of America 0616 FFG
2 4 6 8 10 9 7 5 3 1
Library of Congress Cataloging-in-Publication Data | Names: Styles, Walker, author. | Whitehouse, Ben, illustrator. | Title: Ghosts and goblins and ninja, oh my! / by Walker Styles ; illustrated by Ben Whitehouse. | Description: First Little Simon paperback edition. | New York : Little Simon, 2016. | Series: Rider Woofson ; #4 | Summary: When a team of feline ninja descends upon the animal town of Pawston and the sacred Scroll of Bark-Jitsu disappears, Sensei Hiro, a skilled martial arts sea otter, asks Westie and the rest of the Pup Investigators to investigate. | Identifiers: LCCN 2015038216 | ISBN 9781481463072 (hc) | ISBN 9781481463065 (pb) | ISBN 9781481463089 (eBook) | Subjects: | CYAC: Mystery and detective stories. | Detectives—Fiction. | Dogs—Fiction. | Animals—Fiction. | Martial arts—Fiction. | BISAC: JUVENILE FICTION / Readers / Chapter Books. | JUVENILE FICTION / Action & Adventure / General. | JUVENILE FICTION / Animals / General. | Classification: LCC PZ7.1.S82 Gh 2016 | DDC [Fic]—dc23
LC record available at http://lccn.loc.gov/2015038216

CONTENTS

chapter
ONE

DOJO DOWNER

"Kee-yah!"

The Pawston Martial Arts Dojo was filled with animals practicing their best moves. At the front of the class was Westie Barker, a brilliant terrier with a mind for science. Lately, he was trying to learn the fighting style of Bark-Jitsu.

"*Kee-youch!!!*" Westie shouted again as he hit a plank of wood, but it didn't break.

"You've got this!" the P.I. Pack shouted from the front row. They were sitting with the friends and family of the entire class.

"I hope Westie gets his yellow belt this time around," said Rora Gooddog, one of the smartest detectives in the P.I. game.

"Me too," said Rider Woofson. "Westie has been working very hard."

"Can you believe all the snacks here are *healthy*?" barked Ziggy Fluffenscruff, the youngest member of the team. "They don't have candy or potato chips or anything tasty."

"Do you always think with your stomach, kid?" Rora asked.

"If my tummy is a-rumbling, then I'm a-grumbling," Ziggy replied with a smirk.

"Silence in the dojo, please," said

Sensei Hiro. He was a powerful and skilled martial arts sea otter from the small island of Meowji. Sensei Hiro bowed to his class, and then he bowed to the audience. "Today we celebrate our students as they try to pass the first trial run to earn a yellow belt. The ultimate goal of all young students is to earn their way to the highest black belt,

and thus learn the secrets of the Scroll of Bark-Jitsu."

He bowed toward a statue at the front of the classroom. All of the students bowed to it as well. The large squirrel monkey statue

was the most respected thing in the dojo. In its paws was a single golden scroll.

"Only those who are pure of heart and filled with courage can succeed in the art of Bark-Jitsu,"

said the sensei.
"Let us see who is
worthy."

Westie's paws were sweating.
When the sensei called his name
to go first, Westie became even
more nervous. He took a deep
breath and walked to the start of
the obstacle course.

"Are you ready?" Sensei Hiro
asked.

Westie gulped. "I think so."

"Then, begin!"

Westie ran onto the course. First, he ran up the stairs, but he tripped on the last one and fell over the other side. He got back up. He tried to jump through a set of tires, but his foot got caught on

the first one. The rest of the tires
bounced out of control. The next
part was easy, or so Westie thought.
He tried to weave through a set of
poles, but he went the wrong way.
At the catwalk, his paws were so
sweaty, he slipped off right away.

Then only one obstacle remained:
to grab a bone from the sensei's
hand. Westie jumped for it, but he
missed. He tried four times before
he finally got it. Westie took the

bone and raced toward the finish line.

"I am sorry," Sensei Hiro said, shaking his head. "You did not pass."

With his head down, Westie returned to his friends.

"Hey, pal," Rora said. "I thought you did pretty good."

His other friends agreed, but he knew they were just trying to cheer him up.

"It's harder than it looks, you know," Westie said.

"Really?" Ziggy asked. "It doesn't look hard to that guy."

Westie turned to see that the next student was a cat. The cat ran up the stairs, leaped through the tires, weaved through the poles, darted across the cat-walk, and nabbed the bone on the first try. "Well done, Gato Cato," Sensei Hiro said. "You have earned the yellow belt."

As Gato Cato walked by Westie, he stuck out his tongue. The cat rejoined his friends, some of whom

already had yellow belts. They all
exchanged high-fives.

"Don't worry about it," Rider
said to Westie. "You'll get it next
time, champ."

"Yeah, right," Westie said.

SAFE AND SOUND?

After the belt-giving ceremony, Sensei Hiro waved good-bye to his students and their families and friends. Then he pulled the blinds and locked the door, closing up the dojo for the evening.

The dojo looked just like an ancient temple on the outside. On the inside, though, it had a fancy new security system that was as good as any museum or bank. Sensei Hiro didn't trust any normal system to protect the Scroll of Bark-Jitsu. He spent a lot of money on a high-tech system that could keep the ancient sacred scroll completely safe.

The sensei went to the front door and pulled out a security remote control. He pressed the first button. A tube of

thick glass lowered around the
ancient statue holding the sacred
scroll. The sensei pressed a second
button. The lights went out, and a
grid of laser beams crisscrossed

the entire room. Even more lasers appeared around the glass tube. Then Sensei Hiro pressed the third, and last, button. Nothing seemed to happen, but the sensei knew better.

He plucked a tiny hair from his arm and dropped it on the classroom floor. When the single hair hit the tiles, the floor slid away to reveal a new, more dangerous obstacle course. No

silly thief could make it through that Bark-Jitsu course!

The sensei pressed the last button on the remote control again, and the tiles of the floor slid back over the entire training course, hiding it.

"Stay safe, my sacred Scroll of Bark-Jitsu," the sensei whispered. He bowed one last time to the statue and then locked the door behind him.

The sensei was enjoying his walk home when he

heard something. He looked around the empty street. Across the road was Moose Mikey's Mirror Mall, a large store that sold mirrors of all shapes and sizes. It sounded

like someone had dropped a small mirror inside, but the store was closed.

Sensei Hiro crossed the street and peered in the windows. It was too dark to see anything at first. Suddenly a scary face popped into view. It had a huge hairy nose, pointy ears, green skin, and large red eyes.

"Oh no!" Sensei Hiro cried out. "It cannot be! The ancient Goji Goblin has come for the sacred Scroll of Bark-Jitsu!"

Sensei Hiro—who feared no one in the world—was terrified. He turned around and ran as fast as he could in the other direction.

ATTACK THE SNACK

Back at the P.I. Pack office, Westie carefully stacked dog biscuits into a large pyramid.

"What are you building?" Rora asked, looking over her newspaper.

"I'm not *inventing* anything, if that's what you mean," Westie said. "I'm not in the mood. I need to practice my Bark-Jitsu chop."

"Hey, did someone say pork chop?" Ziggy asked as he sniffed the air.

"No," Westie said as he moved into his attack stance. He took a deep breath, then bowed to the biscuits. He raised his paw, winding it up to bring it down and break the biscuit pyramid in half. "One . . . two . . . three!"

There was a gust of wind, and the biscuits were suddenly gone.

Westie's hand came down on nothing but air. "I think a ghost ate my biscuits!" Westie squeaked.

"There's no such thing as ghosts," Rider said. He pointed at Ziggy, who was crunching loudly in the corner, biscuit crumbs all over his face and paws. "Especially not when there's food near Ziggy."

"*Bow-wowza!* These are good!" Ziggy said, smacking his lips.

"And that's the way the cookie crumbles." Rora grinned.

"Cookies?" Ziggy said.

"Aren't you full?" Rora asked.

"Never!" Ziggy laughed.

"Keep practicing, Westie. I'm sure you'll get that Bark-Jitsu yellow belt before you know it," Rider said. "For now, though, maybe take a break from your new hobby and go back to your old one. We all know you're great when it comes to inventions."

"I do love inventing things," Westie said, smiling for the first time all day. He went to his desk and began to tinker with a mechanical belt. The inside of the belt was covered with tiny wires. "I've been working on something called the Puppy Roller Safety Suit. Just wait until you see what it can do!"

"Can it feed me?" Ziggy asked, wagging his tail.

"No!" Rora rolled up her newspaper and threw it playfully at the young pup.

Ziggy leaped into the air and caught the newspaper in his mouth. Then he tripped and fell, and the newspaper pages went everywhere.

"See? You're not the only clumsy pup in this pack," Rora

said, nodding at Ziggy. Westie smiled.

"Hmm, check this out, Boss," Ziggy said, handing him one of the newspaper pages. "Someone stole a load of mirrors from Moose Mikey's Mirror Mall last night. Seems like an inside job if you ask me. The doors were locked and the video cameras didn't pick up anything. It has the police baffled."

THEFT LAST NIGHT

"Smells like a mystery—" Rider started to say when there was a knock at the door.

Ziggy answered it. "Westie, your sensei is here!" he said.

"Sensei Hiro?" Westie asked. He quickly stood and took a bow. His sensei bowed in return.

Westie bowed again. Then Sensei Hiro bowed.

They took turns bowing until Rora said, "Okay, we get it. You two respect each other. What's up, Sensei?"

"I need your help," Sensei Hiro said. "A terrible curse has come to Pawston, and it is all my fault!"

chapter
FOUR

STORY OF THE
SACRED SCROLL

"I apologize for coming to you, my student," Sensei Hiro said to Westie, "but I did not know where else to turn."

"It's okay, Sensei," Westie said. "I'm glad you came. Please, start at the beginning. We need to know everything."

"This is the story of the sacred

Scroll of Bark-Jitsu, and it is a tale as old as time," the sensei began. "Long, long ago, in ancient Meowji, there was a world of powerful forces, and only those in touch with their inner spirits could calm them. One such animal was a young squirrel monkey. He was a sensei—"

"Like the big statue at your dojo!" Ziggy interrupted.

"Yes," said Sensei Hiro. "The very one."

"*Shhhh,*" Westie hushed his friend.

"One day, the sensei was deep in meditation," Sensei Hiro continued. "Suddenly,

enlightenment struck the young squirrel monkey. He wrote down his thought, for it was perfect and pure. He rolled this thought into a scroll for safekeeping. That night, when he went home, a Goji Goblin was waiting for him. His name was Gus."

"Gus?" Rora said.

"Gus," repeated the sensei. "Gus was very bad, and he demanded the scroll. The young sensei refused. There was a great battle, and after four days of fighting, the sensei won—but at a great

cost! He knew that neither he nor the scroll would be safe anymore, so he took it and ran from his village. The goblin would never give up, not until he had the sacred scroll. So the sensei moved from village to village—around the world—for the rest of his years. Gus the Goji Goblin followed, searching for the scroll. Along the way, the goblin picked up an army of ghosts—"

"Ghosts!" Ziggy and Westie barked. "Scary!"

"There's no such thing," Rider said.

"But there are," said Sensei Hiro. "The young sensei spent his life protecting the scroll. Once he grew old, he passed the sacred text down to his best student. Then it

was the student's duty to protect. This honor was given from generation to generation for hundreds of years until it was passed down to me. I have watched over the scroll for most of my life, and it has always been safe . . . until last night. For I saw the Goji Goblin in the mirror store across from my dojo."

"The Goji Goblin is in Pawston?"

Ziggy and Westie were shocked.

"He is. Will you help me protect the sacred scroll?" Sensei Hiro asked.

"Of course," Westie said, bowing to his sensei. "Protecting the scroll would be an honor."

STEAK-OUT

"I love a good stakeout," Rora said.

"Did you say *steak*?" Ziggy said, his tongue hanging out of his mouth.

"No drooling, Ziggy," Rider said. "We're here to work and help Westie's sensei."

Rider and the P.I. Pack parked their van down the street from the Pawston Martial Arts Dojo. They were watching the building in case someone tried to steal the sacred scroll. "Do you really think Gus the Goji Goblin is trying to steal the Scroll of Bark-Jitsu?" Ziggy asked.

"I do not," said Rider. "I believe a regular bad guy is trying to steal it, and we are going to catch them red-handed."

"But how do you know?" Westie said.

"Because I don't think a goblin

would stop to steal mirrors at a mirror store first. I think someone is getting ready to break into the dojo. They were stealing supplies for the job," Rider said.

"Good catch, Boss," Rora said.

"Just part of a dog detective's work," Rider said. "Now, everyone, into position and remember: Silence is key."

Westie—dressed as a mailbox—took his place across the street from the dojo.

Rora held a pair of binoculars and watched from the van.

Rider—with his collar flipped up and his hat pulled down—took his place under a lamppost, reading the *Pawston Paw Print*.

Ziggy got roof duty on top of the dojo. He brought chips for a snack.

"Everyone is in place," Rider whispered. "Now we wait."

They watched as Sensei Hiro locked up the dojo for the evening.

He walked down the street toward home.

After an hour, nothing had happened. Well, except Ziggy started eating his bag of potato chips, crunching them so loudly that the whole neighborhood could hear. After Rider signaled to him, Ziggy put the chips away, and the quiet waiting continued.

The team waited and waited and waited. Nothing happened until . . .

Woo-woo-woo-woo! Sirens cried as two police cars pulled up.

"Keep your hands where we can see them!" said Frenchie, a French bulldog who had a new job every week. Now he was a police officer.

"Is there a problem, Frenchie?" Rider asked.

"There sure is," Frenchie said. "I'm sorry, Detective, but I need to take you and your friends down to the station for questioning.

Officers, get their van, too. We might need it for evidence."

Rider was always one to obey the law. He got into the police car. So did Rora and Ziggy. The police didn't see Westie dressed up as a mailbox. Rider gave his friend a wink. "We'll be back soon," he whispered to Westie. "Keep watch."

Down at the police station, Rider found the mayor with Mr. Meow.

"Mr. Mayor, what seems to be the problem?" Rora asked.

"A concerned citizen called the police. It seems some snoopy-looking pups

were hanging around the dojo," the mayor said. Rider eyed Mr. Meow. He suspected it was the strange cat who had called the police on the P.I. Pack.

"Let me explain," Rider said. As he told them about working for Sensei Hiro, the mayor and Frenchie listened and nodded.

"Sorry for dragging you down here," Frenchie said. "You're a good detective. I should have known better."

"Don't *ssssay* you're *ssssorry* to him," Mr. Meow said. "His story issss not a *purr*-fectly good reason for him to be lurking around a sssstore."

"If I didn't know better," Rider said, "I'd say Mr. Meow doesn't want us near the dojo right now."

"That is totally absssssurd," the cat hissed angrily. "The mayor ssss-said you're free to go. You're the ones who are sssstill hanging around."

"Then I guess we'll be going," Rider said.

"*Sssstay* out of trouble, detectivessss," Mr. Meow said as the P.I. Pack made their way out the door. Rider wasn't sure why, but he was starting to *not* like that cat.

NIGHT WATCH

While the rest of the P.I. Pack was dealing with the sour*puss* down at the police station, Westie was on his own watching the dojo. He was still dressed up as a mailbox. It was the perfect disguise. No one would notice him—not unless they saw that the mailbox was tiptoe-ing closer and closer to the dojo.

It had been quiet so far, but Westie wanted to make sure. After all, Sensei Hiro had entrusted him to guard the sacred Scroll of Bark-Jitsu. This was a big responsibility. He didn't want to let his sensei down—even if it meant he had to fight a—*gulp!*—goblin and an—*double-gulp!*—army of ghosts!

Suddenly, Westie spotted several black shadows running across a nearby rooftop.

One by one, they darted down a ladder, across an alley, over a fence, and behind some shrubs. Then the black figures gathered in front of the door of the dojo. "Is that *the ghost army?!*" Westie whispered to himself, his nerves making his paws sweat.

One ghost hopped on another's back. Then it pulled out a . . . lock pick.

That's strange, thought Westie. *Why would a ghost need something to unlock a door? Wouldn't it just float right on through?*

The door clicked open, and the five figures darted inside. Westie took a deep breath and crawled across the parking lot as quick as he could to look in through the dojo's window. The ghost army floated up to the ceiling and started moving toward the sacred scroll.

Westie rubbed his eyes, barely able to believe he was seeing ghosts. Though it was rather dark. This gave him an idea. He pulled out one of his inventions— Moon-Glasses! They were like sunglasses, except they helped you see at night. As soon as he put them on,

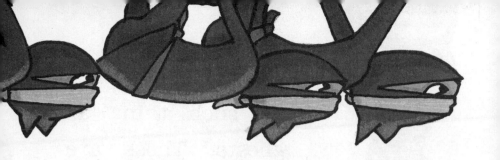

Westie looked back inside the dojo.

"That's no ghost army!" Westie whispered to himself. "Those are ninja!"

The ghosts he thought were floating along the ceiling probably had tails and whiskers, and they were using their claws to crawl across the ceiling so they could avoid walking on the alarmed floor!

"Rider was right," Westie told

himself. "There's no such thing as ghosts. Those are cat burglars!"

The five ninja cats made it across to the other side. Then one by one, the cats held each other's legs. They pulled out small mirrors to divert the lasers safely away as they made a ninja ladder. The alarm wouldn't go off with the mirrors in place. Finally, the bottom cat used his claws to cut a hole in the glass case protecting the scroll, reached inside, and took the scroll.

"This is a major *cat*-tastrophe!" Westie said. "They are stealing the scroll . . . unless . . . unless . . ." Westie had done terribly in

the Bark-Jitsu class. What could *he* do against ninja thieves?

"I am a brilliant inventor and a detective," Westie reminded himself. "And now it's up to *me* to save the scroll!"

chapter
SEVEN

NINJA SHOWDOWN

"Freeze, you naughty ninja cats!" Westie shouted as he kicked open the front door of the dojo.

The ninja cats looked at Westie. They started laughing. "We're not scared of you. You haven't even earned your yellow belt."

"I may not be good at Bark-Jitsu, but I'm good at other stuff."

"Like what?" asked the ninja leader.

"Like stopping bad guys," Westie said with a smile.

He flipped a coin onto the center of the floor. As soon as it landed, it set off the alarm. All of the dojo floor tiles fell away to reveal the new, super–obstacle course underneath.

Surprised by the alarm, the ninja cats tumbled down into the obstacle course. They leaped and jumped, trying to keep from getting trapped by the spinning wheels. A giant hook swung from the ceiling. It almost nabbed the ninja leader, but instead the hook only pulled off his mask.

It was Gato Cato from Westie's class! "You may have set off the alarm," said Gato Cato, "but you still have to catch us!"

"Not a problem." Westie smiled again. He reached down and pushed a button on his mechanical silver belt. "When I'm wearing

the Puppy Roller Safety Suit, nothing can hurt me." The belt buckle opened and blew up a balloon that surrounded Westie. Westie charged forward. As he ran in the puppy ball, it bounced around from danger to danger.

Too bad he couldn't say the same for the ninja cats!

The five cats
tried running and
dodging the ter-
rible obstacles as
best they could. But
one by one, the ninja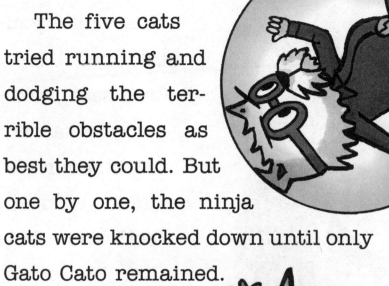
cats were knocked down until only
Gato Cato remained.

"It's just you and me," Gato Cato said, holding the sacred scroll over his head. "And we both know that I'm better at Bark-Jitsu."

"Maybe"—Westie shrugged—"but I'm a better inventor than you!" Westie pulled out a bottle and sprayed the cat's feet. "This morning I invented a superstrong superglue. You won't be getting unstuck from that spot for a long time!"

Sure enough, Gato Cato couldn't move at all.

Westie snatched the scroll from the thief's paw, and held up the scroll proudly. "I believe *this* belongs to Sensei Hiro."

"Are you sure about that?" asked a booming voice. When Westie turned around, he almost screamed like a howler monkey. Gus the Goji Goblin was standing in the doorway. "Give me the scroll."

chapter
EIGHT

GUNG-HO GOBLIN

Westie was shaking in his dog booties. The Goji Goblin Gus blocked the only exit. Smoke was rolling in from outside. "I said, give me the scroll," Gus repeated.

The dog inventor was terrified of the large green creature with pointy ears and a hairy nose, but the scroll belonged to his sensei.

"No," Westie said.

"*No?!*" the goblin roared.

"The sacred Scroll of Bark-Jitsu belongs to Sensei Hiro. And I intend to give it back to him!" Westie ran straight at the goblin. At the last moment, he ducked and slid between the goblin's legs. Once outside, Westie placed the scroll in his mouth and darted toward Central Bark Park. He knew a shortcut through the park to get to the police department, where his friends were.

"You won't escape me!" the goblin

growled. Thunder rumbled as Gus
hopped onto a cloud and began
speeding after Westie. The smoke

was gray, haunting, and sounded
like a loud motorcycle. When the
goblin and his cloud were almost
upon Westie, the inventor pup had
to change tactics. He made a quick
right turn and ducked through a
playground.

Westie ran over a seesaw and

climbed up the slide ladder. The goblin on his cloud went up the other direction and zoomed into the air, swiping the scroll from Westie's mouth.

"Now I've got the scroll!" Gus yelled.

"No, you don't!" Westie pressed

a button on his belt, and the scroll zoomed back into his paw. He had attached a wire to the scroll so he wouldn't drop it—or lose it!

Westie was on the run again. He was almost at the police station when Gus caught up to him on his loud cloud. Gus snatched the scroll, but Westie

wouldn't let go. As they fought, the cloud crashed into an alley. Westie hopped to safety, landing in a delivery truck full of pillows. Gus the Goji Goblin was not so lucky. He crashed into the wall.

"Ouch, *ruff* landing." Westie
snickered.

Gus leaped up, but when he did,
his face was sideways.

"What's wrong with your face?"
Westie asked. "Or is that a *mask*?!"

Gus adjusted it. "No, it's not!" he
barked. "Now give me that scroll!"

Westie was cornered in the alley. There was nowhere to go, but he suspected this goblin was not a goblin at all. If it was just another bad guy, maybe Westie could defeat him with his Bark-Jitsu. Westie took his attack stance.

The goblin shrank back. "You know Bark-Jitsu?"

"I do! Now prepare to meet my furious fist!" Westie said.

The goblin gulped.

Westie ran forward, kicking and chopping the air between him and the goblin. The goblin seemed . . . scared! Westie kept on attacking, but then he slipped in a puddle of oil, which was leaking from the cloud. He flew through the air and landed on his back.

"Good try, ninja pup," the goblin said with a cackle. He took the scroll and snapped the wire attached to Westie's belt. "Thanks for the scroll!"

chapter
NINE

THE GREAT GOBLIN CHASE

Westie watched as the goblin hopped on his cloud and revved its engine. "That's no goblin," Westie said.

Suddenly, a door to the alley opened. "What's all this ruckus out here?" It was Rider Woofson and the rest of the P.I. Pack. The alley was next to the police station!

"Better luck next time, Bark-Jitsu pup!" howled Gus as he raced away.

"A little help, guys?" Westie asked. "That fake goblin has the Scroll of Bark-Jitsu!"

"Jump in the P.I. Pack van,

everyone," Rider said. "The chase is on!"

As the van veered after Gus, Westie quickly told his friends everything that happened after they had left. "I have a hunch that this goblin is not a goblin at all. It's someone wearing a mask!"

"Then how do you explain the cloud he's riding?" Ziggy asked.

"That's no cloud." Rider pointed. The goblin was going so fast that the cloud was fading around him. He was riding a smoking motorcycle!

The cycle-riding goblin was a great driver, but he was no match

for Rora's driving skills. She pulled up beside him. Ziggy and Rider opened the window, and Westie snatched back the scroll.

"Hey! I need that," the goblin shouted, but he wasn't watching

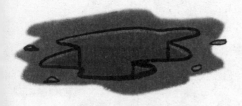

where he was going again, and his front tire hit a pothole. The goblin and the motorcycle both flew into the air and landed in a nearby car wash.

The P.I. Pack pulled over and watched as the goblin was soaped, scrubbed, rubbed, and rinsed through the car wash. When "Gus" came out, his goblin costume was soaked and covered with suds. He could barely move.

"Looks like you're all *washed* up," Ziggy said with a laugh.

"Would you like to do the unmasking, Westie?" Rider asked.

"It would be my pleasure," Westie said. He pulled off the mask. The

entire P.I. Pack gasped. "Rotten Ruffhouse!"

"I should have known," Rider said. "You're up to your no-good tricks again!"

"Game's over!" Ziggy said.

"Not yet!" said Gato Cato and his crew of ninja cats. They quickly stood between the P.I. Pack and Rotten. The dripping wet rottweiler escaped into the darkness with his tail between his legs.

"Westie, did you really think

that you could beat me?" asked
Gato Cato with a laugh. "Now give
us that scroll."

As Gato Cato reached out,
Westie took him by surprise and
flipped the cat over with a perfect

Bark-Jitsu take down! "The scroll belongs to Sensei Hiro!"

The other ninja were about to leap into action when Frenchie and the rest of the police force drove up.

"Not so fast, cats!" said Frenchie.

"Put those paws in the air."

Then Frenchie handcuffed the thieves and tossed them into the back of the police van.

"We've solved another case thanks to you, Westie," Rider said, patting his friend on the back. "I

owe you a congratulations for a job well done."

"You don't owe me anything. It's my honor," Westie said.

"If he doesn't want a reward, I'll take it!" Ziggy barked. "How about a pizza with lots of extra kibble on it?"

chapter
TEN

ALL'S WELL THAT ENDS WELL

The next day, Westie and the P.I. Pack returned the scroll to Sensei Hiro at the Pawston Martial Arts Dojo. He insisted they come in and have some hot green tea. Then he asked Westie to stand in front of the group with him.

"Westie, my student," Sensei Hiro said. "You were very brave in

the face of great danger. You pro-
tected the Scroll of Bark-Jitsu and
stopped the bad guys. To accom-
plish such a feat, you must have
a pure and brave heart. For that,
you deserve this . . ."

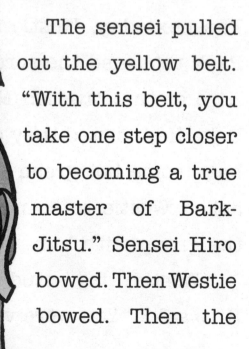

The sensei pulled
out the yellow belt.
"With this belt, you
take one step closer
to becoming a true
master of Bark-
Jitsu." Sensei Hiro
bowed. Then Westie
bowed. Then the

sensei bowed. Then Westie bowed.

"*Dog*gone it! Here we go again."
Ziggy rolled his eyes.

"I am very proud of you," Rider
told his friend after all the bowing
had stopped. "I can't wait to see
you earn your next belt."

"I don't know," Westie said. "Bark-Jitsu is fun, but I'm better at inventing stuff. I think I might stick to that for a while."

"Good call," Ziggy said, pointing at a bowl of boring rice crackers. "Do you think you could invent some better snacks?"

Everyone laughed. Rider shook his head. "Some pups never learn."

Across town in his secret lair, Mr. Meow was hissing at Rotten

Ruffhouse. "You have messsssed up my planssss again! That scroll is worth millions!"

"I'm sorry, Boss," said Rotten, who still had suds in his duds.

Mr. Meow scratched his post.

"I had the police take Rider and his goons away while my ninja cats were supposed to do their business. I planned everything *purr*-fectly. But as always, Rider Woofson foiled me again! Cursssse him!"

"Actually, this time, it was that smart pup, Westie," Rotten noted.

"I am *not* amussssed." Mr. Meow glared at the dog. "One day, I will get that detective, and his puppy pack, too. This issssn't over. . . ."

CHECK OUT RIDER WOOFSON'S NEXT CASE!

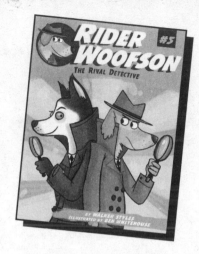

"Pee-yew!" Ziggy Fluffenscruff barked. "This case stinks!"

The Pup Investigators Pack always found themselves in strange spots while solving crimes, but this was their first time in a sewer. They were on the hunt for a stolen wheel of rare aged cheese called the Big Cheddar.

Excerpt from *The Rival Detective*

"Keep sniffing for the cheesy trail," Rider Woofson said. He was the leader of the P.I. Pack and the best dog detective in Pawston.

"*Bow-wowza!* I'm trying. But all I smell is . . . yuck!" the pup said. Ziggy was the youngest member of the Pack, but he had a nose for finding clues.

"Hey, Westie, shine your light this way," said Rora Gooddog. She had a sharp eye for details, even in the dim, dirty sewer.

"Sure thing," Westie Barker said proudly. He pointed a giant helmet

Excerpt from *The Rival Detective*

flashlight toward Rora. The flashlight was his latest invention, and it was a bright idea in the darkness of the tunnel.

"More crumbs," Rora said. "Looks like whoever stole the Big Cheddar stopped for a snack. They left us an actual trail of bread crumbs."

"Ugh," Ziggy said with watery eyes. "I can't believe I'm saying this, but I think I've lost my appetite. That's how bad it stinks down in this place."

Excerpt from *The Rival Detective*